WHAT'S MY SCORE?

A Fun Exercise in the Rules of Golf

Steve McCall

First Edition

PAGE PUBLISHING, INC.
New York, NY

First originally published by Page Publishing, Inc. 2017

ISBN 978-1-64027-572-0 (Paperback)
ISBN 978-1-64027-573-7 (Digital)

Printed in the United States of America

PREFACE

I have been in awe with the game of golf ever since I can remember. Every aspect of it, from the pristine confines of the course itself to the rules that command their respect. I am also amazed at the solidarity of its self-imposed honor code and surprised at all the intricacies of its guideline.

Ever since my father told me keep silent while a pro was putting (mind you, we were watching the television), I have had this desire and fondness for the game.

Please follow as our competitor, Steve, plays in a club-sponsored tournament and try to determine if the score he marked on his scorecard is correct. He thinks they are—it is up to you verify his score. He may be right—it is your mission to get it correct!

ACKNOWLEDGMENTS

Special thanks to:
Sue Salit.
Steve "Koson" Koscs.
Golf Professional Bill Galloway.
Mr. Kyle Krahl for the illustrations.
D. Jill Schmid–Publicity Photo
My family for allowing me to share this game with them.
Jane and David for all the great rounds we shared.

READING GUIDE

1. A hole-by-hole account of a fictitious person (Steve) playing in a tournament at his local club.
2. A scorecard with what score Steve presumes he has.
3. A scorecard with what Steve really scored—reality.
4. The rule that applied to that situation.
5. A description of the rule breached, and why it was breached, in stroke-play format.

The rules and comments in this exercise are not intended to be an interpretation of the rules of golf by the United States Golf Association (USGA). These comments are purely an effort to generate thought and to encourage players to acquire a working knowledge of the rules. Opinions on the outcome of situations in this book are from a person who holds no accreditation to any governing body with the USGA.

Please note that many times in this book, there are references to the terms "pin" and "trap"; these are common terms that are not recognized by the official rules. They are referred to as "flagstick" and "bunker" respectively.

What's My Score?

SCORECARD

Hole	1	2	3	4	5	6	7	8	9	Out	10	11	12	13	14	15	16	17	18	Back	Front	Total
Blue Tee	410	424	512	175	469	501	316	110	454		406	414	379	511	180	438	555	149	435			
Steve																						
Reality																						
What You Think He Got																						
Par	4	4	5	3	4	5	4	3	4	36	4	4	4	5	3	4	5	3	4	36	36	72

Date ______________ Scorer ______________________ Attest ______________________

HOLE #1

Par 4
410 Yards

As I stand on the tee, looking all around
I try to look composed as I put my tee into the ground
My nerves are a wreck, thank you, Juan Valdez
My mind runs a checklist like a game of Simon Says.

I somehow make the swing and hit that shiny ball
I've hit it straight, I've hit it long, and if that isn't all
I hit the furthest, a first time for that,
Usually I hit it in the rough or, better, hit it fat!

My approach shot is hit quite crisp, like those back at the range
Five feet away—time to mark it as I fumble for some change
I'm feeling pretty confident, my mouth I cannot shut
For I will start with birdie three if I make this putt.

I grab my putter then notice all fourteen clubs there in my bag
And discover there's an extra one still sporting a price tag
As I lift it up, I see affixed a note
"To you my, loving husband" is all that my wife wrote!

So glad that I discovered that before my putt was holed
Because I would have had to add two strokes, and my wife I would have sold!
But as luck turns out, I made my birdie 3
And declared that new club out of play, what a start for me!

Steve: 3
Par: 4

14 OR 15

HOLE # 1

Par 4

What Steve thinks he got: 3
What he really got: 5
Why: Due to Rule 4-4a, maximum of fourteen clubs. The player must not start a stipulated round with more than fourteen clubs.

Note that this rule has *some* forgiveness to it. The penalty is two strokes for each hole at which any breach occurred. Maximum penalty per round, four strokes. So if discovered after you tee off on the first hole, penalty of two strokes. If you noticed your infraction on, say, on the sixteenth hole you would only add two stokes for the first two holes—maximum four strokes!

These things happen. It is a good habit to clean your clubs before you play so you can count them as a precaution.

Match Play: At the conclusion of the hole at which the breach is discovered, the state of the match is adjusted by deducting for each hole at which the breach occurred; maximum deduction per round: two holes.

HOLE # 2

Par 4
424 yards

To birdie the first hole is a very awesome treat
And having "honors" is indeed a humble feat
It's like "king of the hill" being "A" number one
And to keep said "honors" is just as half the fun!

I bring back my club, and the ball it surely goes
And where it ends up, nobody knows
I pulled it just a little as I watch and fret
For where this ball is heading I believe it will be wet.

My fears are justified as I have found a winding brook
Just *beyond* the red stakes, my confidence is shook
I will hit from here—all in all, a risky shot
I sole my club behind the ball and give it all I've got!

I hit it well, and the mud it sure did fly
But I gotta tell ya, that I am happy with that try
It lands on the green not too far away
A straight putt will do if it doesn't stray.

Left it on the lip, that's a common sight
If my putter keeps this up, it soon may take a flight.
But a four on that hole isn't all that bleak
On to the next hole, more birdies I shall seek!

Steve: 4
Par: 4

HOLE # 2

Par 4

What Steve thinks he got: 4
What he really got: 6
Why: Due to Rule 13-4 (b), ball in hazard.

Except as provided in the rules, before making a stroke at a ball that is in a hazard (whether a bunker or water hazard), the player must not do the following:

A) Test the condition of the hazard or any similar hazard
B) Touch the ground in the hazard or the water in the water hazard with his hand or club
C) Touch or move a loose impediment lying or touching the hazard

Penalty: two strokes—ouch!

Try and remember that the stakes—be they red, yellow or white—are a warning system. Think of them as snakes! As soon as he put his club on the ground in the red-staked area, he was in trouble. Unfortunately, our poor player is not off to such the start he thought he was!

Match Play: Loss of hole.

HOLE # 3

Par 5
512 Yards

After two holes, I am one under par
I hope I can say that when I am safe in the bar!
Try and stay upbeat, have a good swing thought
That's all I recall from all the lessons I've bought.

After an errant drive, I am in a familiar spot
At first glance, I don't have a shot
I'm stuck under a branch without a clear swing
I bend the branch back so I can hit that darn thing!

Advance the ball, that was my goal
And two more shots, I'm two feet from the hole
I make the putt and put a 5 on my card
I really don't know why this game is so hard.

Steve: 5
Par: 5

HOLE # 3

Par 5

What Steve thinks he got: 5
What Steve really got: 7
Why: Breach of Rule 13-2, Improving lie, area of intended stance or swing, or line of play.

A player must not improve or allow to be improved:

- The position or lie of his ball
- The area of his intended stance or swing (bending the branch back)
- His line of play or a reasonable extension of that line beyond the hole
- The area in which he intends to drop the ball.

Penalty: two strokes.

Remember, the old adage "Play the course the way you found it" comes in to play here. Just remember that you really can't move much of anything until you are on the green. When it comes to moving things, ask your playing companions.

Steve thought he got a par, but he has to add the two-stroke penalty.

There is an old adage I hear whenever I am in precarious situations: "Avoid the appearance of evil!"

Match Play: Loss of hole.

HOLE # 4

Par 3
175 yards

Although I made par, my opponent made a "bird"
He's hitting first, now I'm hitting third
This distance is troubling what club should I pick?
It's either a 6 or a 7; I can't decide on the stick.

As my opponent begins to address his tee shot
I look into his bag to see which club he has got
He is hitting his "7," for I see his "6" and his "8"
My confidence grows stronger, I can hardly wait!

My turn to hit, my "bravado" is brewing
I feel like a pro, with a gallery viewing
Right over the flagstick and safely on the pad
One of the least painful of pars that I've ever had.

Steve: 3
Par: 3

HOLE # 4

Par 3

What Steve thinks he got: 3
What he really got: 3
Why: Due to Rule 8-1 Advice, indicating line of play. During a stipulated round, a player must not:

A) Give advice to anyone in the competition playing on the course other than his partner
B) Ask for advice from anyone other than his partner or either of their caddies

Penalty: two strokes

Since Steve did not ask which club he was using, he is not in breach of this rule.

If Steve had moved, say, a towel to see what clubs he was using, then he would be in breach—but just looking is okay.

No penalty.

Match Play: No penalty.

HOLE # 5

Par 4
469 yards

I like the way this hole sets up for me
Pretty straight, two bunkers, and not even one tree
I bring back my driver and swing like a young Rory
The ball's in the fairway and not in the quarry.

I arrive at my ball, and my smile is erased
For now I have a challenge that I've never faced.
My ball is an inch behind a fairway drain
This game is becoming such a pain.

It's not on it but pretty darn near
I don't want to hit it and that is my fear—
I know this rule, and I can't take relief
Because it's not on it, well that's my belief!

I swing like a champ and muscle it through
Not a great shot and now I lay "two"
Two more shots, and now I am done
I got my par 4, but it wasn't much fun.

Steve: 4
Par: 4

125 Yards
To Hole

HOLE # 5

Par 4

What do you think Steve got?
What Steve thinks he got: 4
What Steve really got: 4

Well, in this instance, it would have helped Steve if he *did* know the rules—in this case Rule 24-2, immovable obstruction.

> A) Interference
>
> Interference by an immovable obstruction occurs when a ball lies in *or* on the obstruction, or when the obstruction interferes with the player's stance or his intended swing.

Steve could have gotten relief without penalty, within one club length of and not nearer the hole than the nearest point of relief.

Meaning that you mark it with a tee then get full relief with your stance (not nearer to the hole) and take a drop within the one club length.

If you think you will get hurt on any swing, ask for help.

* USGA Rules of Golf
** Decisions on the Rules of Golf.

Match Play: Since there was no rule breached, no penalty.

HOLE # 6

Par 5
501 Yards

I hit this so perfectly, I quickly grab my wrist
My pulse is 150, I think a beat has been missed
I take a stroll and survey my position
Being in the fairway is good for my condition.

Naturally my approach shot is off just a smidge
Lying over a hazard smack in the middle of a bridge
A precarious situation, now what do I do?
I can take a drop or hit it; the options are quite few.

Can I ground my club? That is my concern
I should have my rule book; someday I will learn.
I take a guess and ground the club, then take a cautious pass
And luck be with me as it finds the short grass!

The ball looks so pretty sitting by the pin
And to make that shot looks so easy makes me want to grin
A tap-in birdie or at least that's what I pray
I mark a four on my card and head off on my way.

Steve: 4
Par: 5

HOLE # 6

Par 5

What Steve thinks he got: 4
What Steve really got: 4
Why: Due to Rule 13-4 (exception 30) Ball in Hazard; Prohibited Actions.

A bridge is an obstruction. In a hazard, the club may touch an obstruction at address or in the backward movement for the stroke—see note under Rule 13-4. Touching the bridge prior to address is also permissible, since an obstruction in a water hazard is not "ground in the hazard."

This applies even if the bridge has been declared an integral part of the course.

In this case, Steve incurs no penalty since he was on an obstruction.

Match Play: No penalty.

HOLE # 7

Par 4
316 Yards

Playing what I feel is the round of my career
I blister a drive that even Tiger would cheer
It's definitely the best that I have ever seen
My opponents mumble, "You're ten feet from the green!"

When I arrive at my ball, it's then that I observe
That I'm in some deep rough, this lie I don't deserve.
One foot from the short grass doesn't seem quite fair
My visions of an easy bird have vanished into thin air.

I take my stance and get ready to hit
I'm at the top of my backswing and the ball moves a bit.
I quickly readjust and just like Mickelson, Phil
Plop that baby on the green, let's go for the kill!

I stroke the putt softly then watch it start to roll
The strain this game has on you is starting to take its toll
But thank you, Mr. Luck, and the laws of gravity
My birdie putt occupies that once vacant cavity.

Steve: 3
Par: 4

HOLE # 7

Par 4

What Steve thinks he got: 3
What Steve really got: 4
Why: Due to Rule 18-2, ball at rest moved.
B. Ball Moving After Address.

If a player's ball in play moves after he has addressed it (other than as a result of a stroke), the player is deemed to have moved the ball and incurs a penalty of one stroke. The ball must be replaced, unless the movement of the ball occurs after the player has begun the stroke (like Steve) or the backward movement of the club for the stroke and the stroke is made.

Penalty: one stroke.

Once again, play the ball from where you find it. If it moves and you caused it, it will most likely be a penalty.

Just a note, if you ground your club and the ball moves, you must put the ball back and take a 1-stroke penalty. If you don't move the ball back, you now have played from wrong place and subsequently take another 1-stroke penalty. (Total of two strokes ... ouch!)

Match Play: Loss of hole.

HOLE # 8

Par 3
110 Yards

The shortest hole that I will play today
110 yards and straight away
Not much trouble to avoid, only a sand pit
And of course I have found the center of it.

My face reveals my discovery
My ball's in a puddle—need a miracle recovery!
For I know that I must play where she lay
And sometimes the rules can ruin your day.

But the rules only attempt to make this game fair
And for that fact alone I must play it from there.
So like the fool that I am, I deliver a powerful swing
Only to notice I haven't moved the darn thing!

The ball hasn't moved, and I am soaking wet
I now lay two, not out of this yet
After four more swings, I get the ball to migrate
And two-putt myself into a memorable eight.

Steve: 8
Par: 3

HOLE # 8

Par: 3

What Steve thinks he got: 8
What Steve really got: 8
Why: Due to Rule 25, abnormal ground conditions, embedded ball and wrong putting green.

25-1 b. Relief: Except when the ball is in a hazard or lateral hazard, a player may take relief from interference by an abnormal ground condition as follows:

- ii) In a Bunker: If the ball is in a bunker, the player must lift the ball and drop it either:
  - a) Without penalty: to the nearest point of relief and the ball must be dropped in the bunker or, if complete relief is impossible, as near as possible to the spot where the ball lay, but not nearer the hole, on a part of the course in the bunker that maximum available relief from the condition.*

No penalty.
It's okay to ask for a little help out there.
This one really cost Steve some momentum!

Match Play: No penalty. (Hopefully your opponent will know the rule and offer some help... it's only fair!)

* USGA Rules of Golf

HOLE # 9

Par 4
454 Yards

Great hole that was! No more honors for me
A "snowman" on my scorecard, I'm the last on the tee
It was fun while it lasted, I was under par
Now I am over. I should head right to my car!

But golf is a game of famine or feast
I could turn this around, give it a try at least!
My drive's in the middle at the 100-yard post
From here I can birdie, make par at the most.

I arrive at my ball and swing effortlessly
This one looks good, but how good will it be?
Two feet from the pin is where it ends up
And soon it will be resting at the bottom of the cup.

I tidy the area where my ball came to rest
Tap those cleat marks down and put my putter to test.
Never an easy putt, that is what I have been told
But this one was stuck true, solid and bold.

Steve: 3
Par: 4

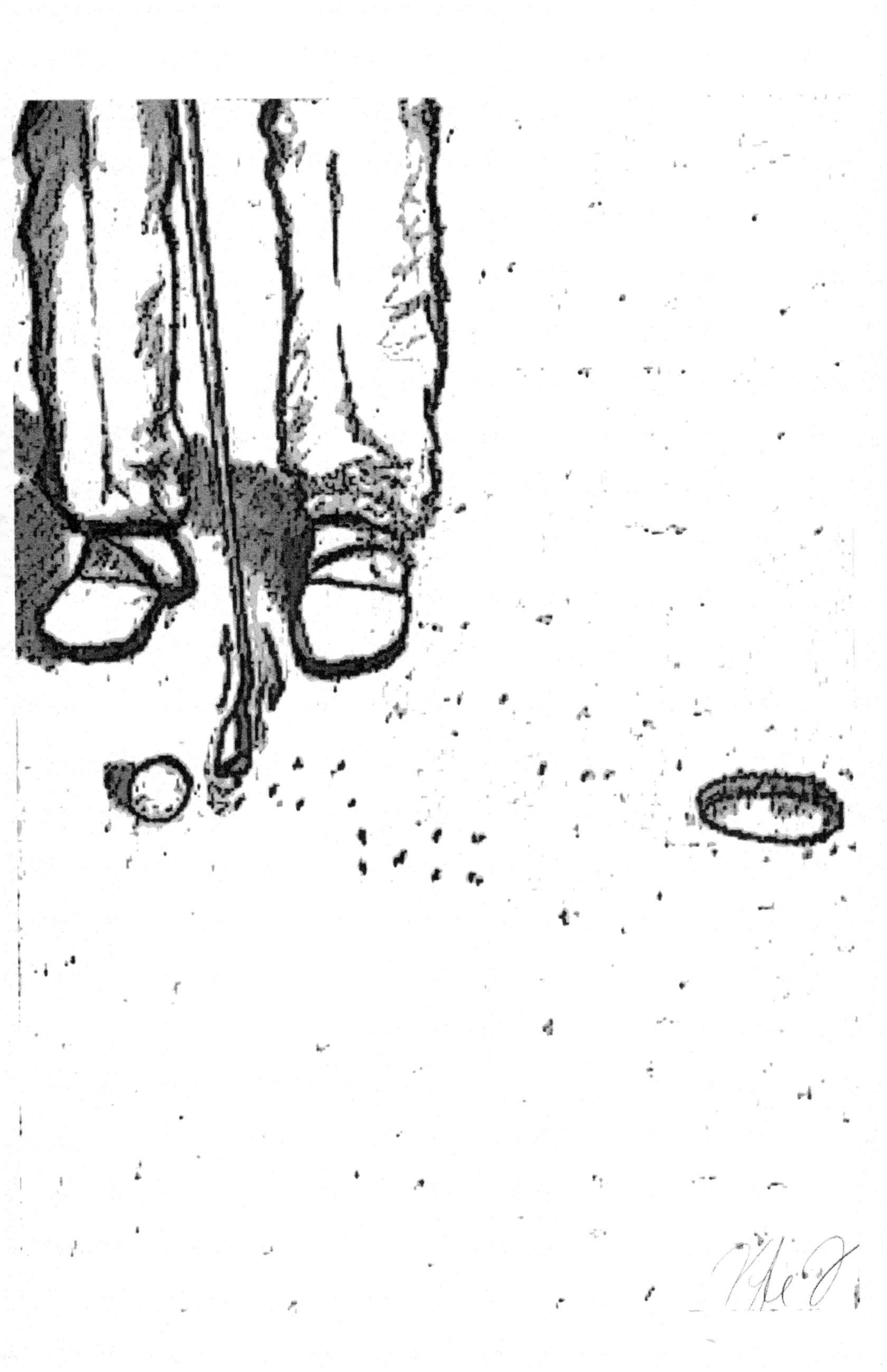

HOLE # 9

Par 4

What Steve thinks he got: 3
What Steve really got: 5
Why: Due to Rule 16-1 (a), touching line of putt.

The line of putt must not be touched except:

a) The player may remove loose impediments, provided he does *not press anything down:*

Penalty: two strokes.

Unfortunately, poor Steve tamped down the spike marks that were in his line—big no no—I wouldn't tamp down any even if they *weren't* in the line

Things you can fix:

1. Any ball mark.
2. An old hole plug (left by replacing a hole)
3. *Loose* impediments, i.e., twigs.

You can also place your putter in front of ball at address so long as you don't press down.

Match Play: Loss of hole.

HOLE # 10

Par 4
406 yards

Nine holes down with just nine more to go
I may be in contention, hey, ya never know!
While the others go in to grab a little bite
I'll hit some balls as I don't want to get tight.

After a bucket, it's off to number 10
I haven't been this loose in God knows when.
I smash the ball into the midday sun
This game is so crazy, it's almost fun!

With the touch of a lumberjack, I skull the approach
And begin to look around for my coach.
But with "MacGyver"-like skills, I muster a four
And after that, "skull job" isn't such a bad score!

Steve: 4
Par: 4

HOLE # 10

Par 4

What Steve thinks he got: 4
What Steve really got: 6
Why: Due to Rule 7-2, practice, during round.

Penalty: 2 Strokes

Rule 7-2: A player must not make a stroke during play of a hole.

Between the play of two holes, a player must not make a practice stroke, except that he may practice putting or chipping on or near:

- The putting green of the last hole played
- Any practice putting green, or
- The teeing ground of the next hole played in the round.

(Provided a practice stroke is not made form a hazard *and does not unduly delay play!)*

In stroke play, I wouldn't chance practicing anywhere on the course that you are currently playing. The chances are too great that you may be doing something which will add to your score.

Match Play: Loss of hole. (In this case, the hole you are about to play.)

HOLE # 11

Pa4 4
414 Yards

Things were looking good as I teed off on 11
That's when I got my gift from heaven
It happened as my approach lay safely on the green
And a miracle occurred like one I've never seen.

My opponent's shot was tracking towards my ball
It crashed right into mine, and if that is not all
Right into the cup! There was nothing left to do
Except to mark on down my score of an eagle-two!

But as I walked to the next tee
Something very eerie came over me
I tell the boys I think I have done something wrong
And I'm going back, won't be long!

I yell to the foursome behind to wait just a bit
"I'll be out of the way soon, then you can hit."
I put the ball back where it used to be
And proceed to make the putt for what is now a birdie three!

Steve: 3
Par: 4

HOLE # 11

Par 4

What Steve thinks he got: 3
What Steve really got: 3
Why: Due to Rule 18-5, ball at rest moved.

Penalty: no penalty. If he did not move it back, he would have been in trouble as he would have put down an inaccurate score: 2.

Then he would've been in trouble at the end of the round for scoring an incorrect scorecard (Rule 6-6).

There are some funny things that happen on a golf course, and don't forget you can always act like you don't know and ask later. Tell your competitors that you will drop a ball as a provisional and put down both the eagle and the birdie and ask your pro before signing your card!

Match Play: No penalty.

HOLE # 12

Par 4
379 Yards

Once again the "honors" are all mine
I'm standing at one under par on this final nine.
The hole is straight as an arrow—trouble on the right.
I "smoke" my drive and marvel at its flight.

Eighty yards to the flag is now what I face
I hit my approach, my hearts builds up to maximum pace.
Into another bunker, this game is so annoying
This is the type of fun that I'm really not enjoying!

I reach the crime scene only to discover
The rake is so close to my ball, you'd think that it was his lover!
How can I move this rake without moving my ball?
For I am in a bunker and can't move the ball at all.

I'll take a drop and add one penalty stroke
And thoughts of a great round have turned into a joke
On the green after, I make a mighty cut
And score myself a bogey five after I make the putt.

Steve: 5
Par: 4

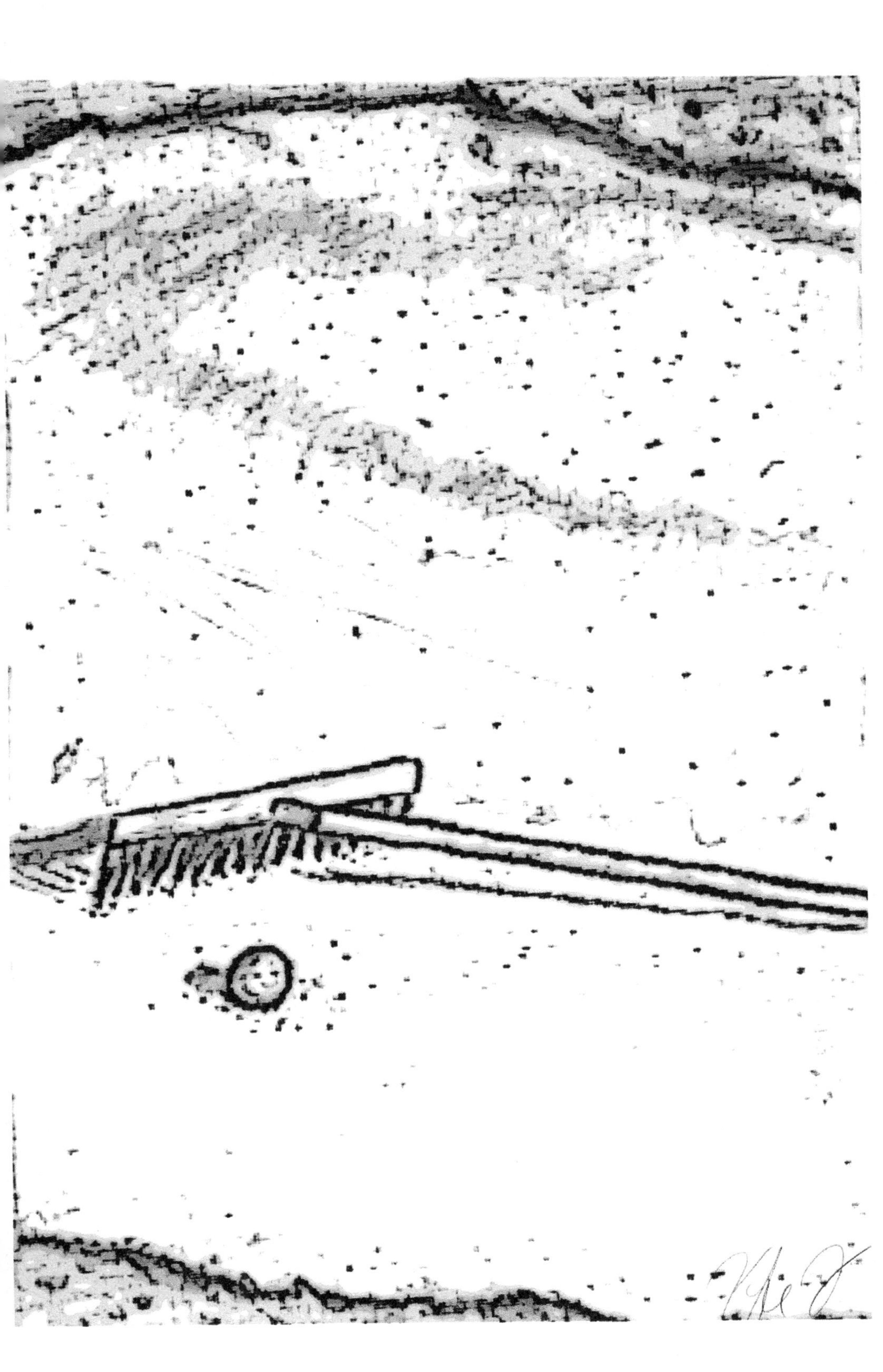

HOLE # 12

Par 4

What Steve thinks he got: 5
What Steve really got: 5
Why: Due to Rule 24, obstructions (24-1, movable obstruction).

A player may take relief, *without penalty*, from a movable obstruction as follows:

a) If the ball does not lie on the obstruction, the obstruction may be removed.
b) If the ball moves, there is no penalty, provided that the movement of the ball is directly attributable to the removal of the obstruction.*

Well, that one is pretty simple! Don't be afraid to ask your competitors for these type of rulings. Great to have a rulebook with you as well.

This was another stroke that could have been avoided.

What Steve could have done was move the obstruction (the rake), and if the ball didn't move, he was fine. If the ball moved after he removed the rake, he would have no penalty and will replace his ball in its original spot.

Match Play: No penalty.

* USGA Rules of Golf

HOLE # 13

Par 5
511 Yards

Six holes left, time to make a move
Seems like in tournament play, I never find my groove
Hit away, hit the ball, put it into play
It's time to stop thinking, "It's just another day!"

Lying two by the green under a knarly pine
The branches so low they creep all up my spine.
Go underneath, get on my knees for I have no stance
I kneel on my towel, don't want to stain my pants!

Always have to be thinking in order to stay in it
And that's what I have to do if I'm going to win it!
I'll take a birdie from underneath that tree
Moving on to the next hole happy as can be!

Steve: 4
Par: 5

HOLE # 13

Par 5

What Steve thinks he got: 4
What Steve really got: 6
WHY: Due to Rule 13, ball played as it lies.

The ball must be played as it lies, except as otherwise provided in the *rules.*

Specifically 13-2

A player must not improve or allow to be improved:

- The position or lie of his ball.
- The *area* of his intended *stance* or swing-

This will have a penalty of two strokes.

This is the same thing that happened to Mr. Craig Stadler at the 1987 San Diego Open, when he put a towel on the ground to protect his expensive pants from getting messy. Unfortunately he did sign his card and was later penalized the two strokes, thus being disqualified for signing the wrong score. That cost him $37,000, which is way more costly than a pair of pants.

Match Play: Loss of hole.

HOLE # 14

Par 3
180 Yards

Alas, I find myself again at a par three
They look so darn easy for the flag I clearly see!
But they can turn on you, and awfully quick, my friend
And it will be the par three standing in the end.

'Tis only 180 yards, no wind that I can feel
The club feels like a jackhammer as I've hit it on the heel
It's heading out of bounds, this one will be tight.
These are the shots I lose sleep on each and every night!

I arrive to discover my faith strengthened by the Lord
My ball is inbounds by an inch, no less no more!
Just a small issue, as I cannot make a swing
For the white stakes in my way—I'll just move that stupid thing.

I pull out that stake, and it comes out with such ease
And my next shot is so gorgeous, it brings me to my knees
The game of my life, this is definitely my day!
As I tap in for an easy par, things are going my way.

Steve: 3
Par: 3

HOLE # 14

Par 3

What Steve thinks he got: 3
What Steve really got: 5
Why: Due to Rule 13-2, ball played as it lies.

13-2, improving lie, area of intended stance or swing, or line of play.

A player must not improve or allow to be improved:

- Moving, bending, or breaking anything growing or fixed (including immovable obstructions and objects defining out of bounds.)

Penalty: two strokes.
Ironically, you can move yellow or red stakes!
Steve is not having a great day!

Match Play: Loss of hole.

HOLE # 15

Par 4
438 Yards

The countdown begins, four holes left to play
This has certainly been a most exciting day.
And after two shots, I lay upon the fringe
With a sidewinder putt that would make anybody cringe!

I ask my opponent "Please remove the *stick*"
Then proceed to "skull" my putt; I've hit it like a brick.
It's moving toward the flagstick left upon the green
And then I witness something rarely seen-

Marty, my opponent, has turned into my ally
And picks up that darn flagstick as the ball goes whizzing by.
This man is now my hero; he must have a good soul
For I make the long putt, and the ball rests in the hole!

Steve: 4
Par: 4

HOLE # 15

Par 4

What Steve thinks he got: 4
What Steve really got: 4
Why: Due to Rule 1-2, exerting influence on the ball.

A player or caddie must not take any action to influence the position or the movement of a ball except in accordance with the rules!

Removal of movable obstruction (in this case, flagstick on the green) —Rule 24-1

Years ago, Marty's actions would have put him in trouble, as you weren't allowed to move things on the green!

No penalty!

Match Play: No penalty.

HOLE # 16

Par 5
555 Yards

The last of the five-pars, this one is very long
But the winds at my back, and, baby, it's strong
Winning today would be a bad bet with my bookie
But "choking" is a sure bet; at that, I am no rookie!

I hit driver from the fairway and hit it very well
After sixteen holes, I think I'm beginning to gel!
My ball's on the dance floor, and I'm feeling mighty regal
Twenty feet to the hole, can I please manage an eagle?

I bend my large carcass to mark my little ball
And accidently move the ball, but not much at all
So I move the ball back to its original place
And go about the challenge that I currently face.

I actually see the line that I have to take
This putt to me looks like a piece of cake
With Crenshaw-like feel, I stroke upon that sphere
And with eager anticipation, watch it disappear!

Steve 3
Par 5

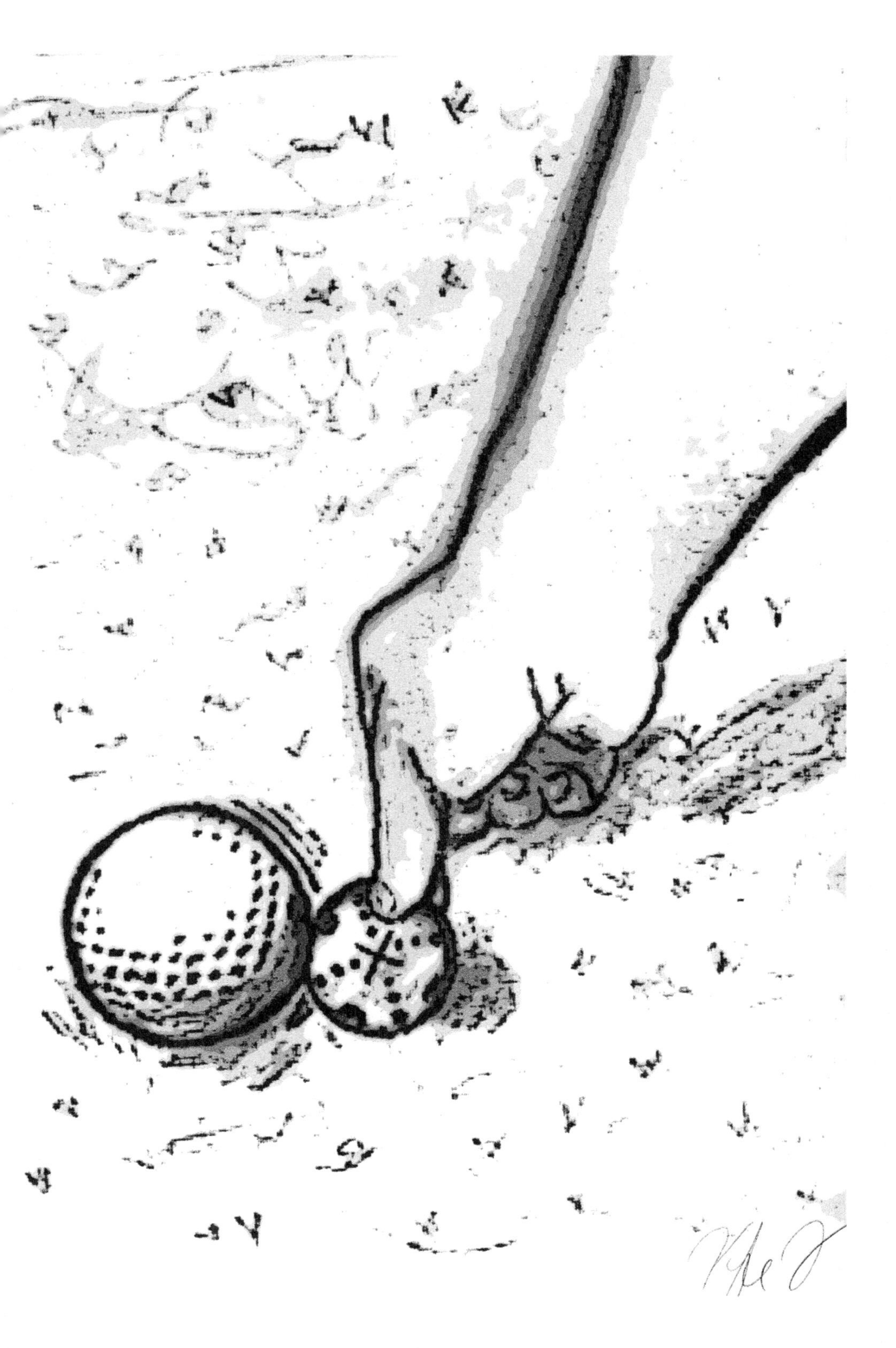

HOLE # 16

Par 5

What Steve thinks he got: 3.
What Steve really got: 3.
Why? Due to Rule 20-1. Lifting, dropping and placing; playing from wrong place.

The position of the ball must be marked before it is lifted under a rule that requires it to be replaced. If a ball or ball marker is *accidentally* moved in the process of lifting the ball under a rule or marking its position, the ball or ball marker must be replaced. There is no penalty, provided the movement of the ball or ball marker is directly attributable to the specific act of marking the position of or lifting the ball.*

Penalty: no penalty.

Since Steve did the right thing and put the ball back to its original position and then marked the ball.

Match Play: No penalty.

* USGA Rules of Golf: Rule 20-1

HOLE # 17

Par 3
149 Yards

I tee my ball with a stubble of a tee
Because that's what the pros do (I've seen it on TV)
Intentionally I fade the ball, at least that what I say
And my ball finds the green, yes, and my lucky day!

A downhill putt that's merely six feet in length
I stroke at the ball, but does it have the strength?
The ball is rolling, heading for that abyss
And it stops on the edge, a heartbreaking near miss

In utter frustration, I stomp my feet upon the ground
And quickly hear *ker-chink*—man, I love that sound.
So instead of settling for a par, I have netted me a "bird"
Now I only have one hole to go, this game is so absurd!

Steve: 2
Par: 3

HOLE # 17

Par 3

What Steve thinks he got: 2
What Steve really got: 4
Why? Due to Rule 1, the game.

Rule 1-2: A player or caddie must not take *any* action to influence the position of the ball, except in accordance with the rules!*

Penalty: two strokes

The stomping of his feet so close to the ball on the edge had an obvious effect on the ball falling in. I bet if he had waited his allowed ten seconds, the ball may have fallen in all by itself. Gravity is a powerful force.

Match Play: Loss of hole.

* USGA Rules of Golf.

HOLE # 18

Par 4
435 Yards

The last hole finds me humbled and a wee bit sad
That should be expected with the round that I have had.
Eager to put to a round that became bizarre
And enjoy an adult beverage at the local bar.

After a fairly good drive, I hit shot number 2
But Marty says, "You hit out of turn," now what do I do?
He tells me to just add a stroke to my final score
I guess he who was once a friend is no friend to me no more!

I shake the mass that holds my hat in utter disbelief
And when I die, it's the rule book that I shall bequeath!
I tap in my putt that would have been a par
Then add my penalty and drudge off to my car.

I turn in my scorecard to the scorer's table
Words try to escape my mouth, but find they are unable.
The vision of a win today is forgotten, but only for awhile
As I will be back on the tee tomorrow and wearing me a SMILE!

Steve 5
Par 5

HOLE # 18

Par 4

What Steve thinks he got: 5
What Steve really got: 4
Why? Rule 10, order of play.
No penalty!

10-2 Stroke Play c) Playing out of turn: If a player plays out of turn, there is no penalty. If, however, the committee determines the competitors have agreed to play out of turn to give one of them an *advantage, they are disqualified*!*

So a par after all! The rules are supposed to make the game easier and fair to all—sometimes they are very difficult to grasp. In this era of instant access, you can easily look things up with your phones. If not, play two balls or jot down your issues and talk with the pro!

Match Play: If a player plays when his opponent should have, there is no penalty, but the opponent may immediately require the player to cancel the strokes so made and, in correct order, play a ball as nearly as possible at the spot from which the original ball was last played—in this case re-teeing.

Well, what a round of golf. I hope you enjoyed yourself and got your mind to think about situations that can occur in any golf round.

How did you do? What a difference. Steve's card nets him a score of 70; but according to the rules, he really had 86! How can that be? Then he would have been disqualified for signing a wrong score!

I know this is a drastic example of a round of golf, but I have experienced or been in a group where all of these situations have happened.

I encourage you to get on the USGA's website and hit the rules tab. Better yet, join the USGA and become a member. It's the best game around. Enjoy!

ABOUT THE AUTHOR

Steve McCall's love of the game of golf can be blamed on his mother, Jane. As a coordinator for Junior League, she made certain Steve was taught the proper etiquette of this gentlemen's sport. At the age of nine, he built a two-hole course in the green area behind his house and imagined that Pat Summerall was calling his shots. At the age of twelve, Steve had the opportunity to caddy for his mother in her weekly Syracuse district events. He learned that, on this higher level of play, the rules of golf during a competition become much more important. As a caddy, it was necessary that he understood the scoring rules or it could cost his mother her match. Steve practiced his game whenever he could. His passion for the sport and his competitive nature earned him the title of captain for both his high school and college teams. After college, he enjoyed club events and earned the President's Cup and Club Championship at his home course, Beaver Meadows in Phoenix, NY. With all that experience behind him, he began to understand that these rules aren't meant to punish but to help every player have the same "equal footing" in this difficult sport.

CPSIA information can be obtained
at www.ICGtesting.com
Printed in the USA
LVOW03s0551071117
555222LV00003B/486/P